DISNEY'S
TOONTOWN

Mickey's
Twelve Days of
Christmas

Adapted by Margaret Snyder
Illustrated by Darrell Baker

©Disney Enterprises, Inc.

MERRIGOLD PRESS® • NEW YORK

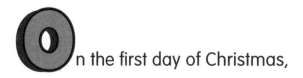

On the first day of Christmas,

Goofy gave to me

A partridge in a square tree.

On the second day of Christmas,

Minnie gave to me

Two dancing gloves,

And a partridge in a square tree.

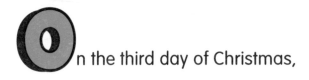

On the third day of Christmas,

Donald gave to me

Three feather pens,

Two dancing gloves,

And a partridge in a square tree.

On the fourth day of Christmas,

Scrooge gave to me

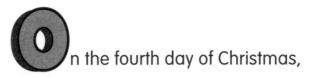

Three feather pens,

Two dancing gloves,

And a partridge in a square tree.

On the fifth day of Christmas,

Morty gave to me

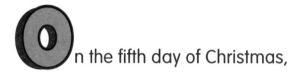

Four crawling worms,

Three feather pens,

Two dancing gloves,

And a partridge in a square tree.

On the sixth day of Christmas,

Ferdie gave to me

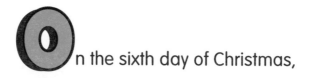

Five windup things,

Four crawling worms,

Three feather pens,

Two dancing gloves,

And a partridge in a square tree.

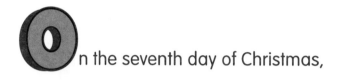

On the seventh day of Christmas,

Pluto gave to me

Seven balls a-bouncing,

Six cars a-zooming,

Five windup things,

Four crawling worms,

Three feather pens,

Two dancing gloves,

And a partridge in a square tree.

On the eighth day of Christmas,

Daisy gave to me

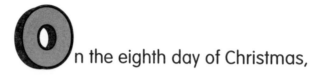

Seven balls a-bouncing,

Six cars a-zooming,

Five windup things,

Four crawling worms,

Three feather pens,

Two dancing gloves,

And a partridge in a square tree.

On the ninth day of Christmas,

Huey gave to me

Nine spiders spinning,

Eight flowers singing,

Seven balls a-bouncing,

Six cars a-zooming,

Five windup things,

Four crawling worms,

Three feather pens,

Two dancing gloves,

And a partridge in a square tree.

On the tenth day of Christmas,

Dewey gave to me

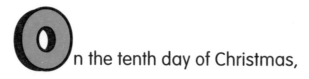

Nine spiders spinning,

Eight flowers singing,

Seven balls a-bouncing,

Six cars a-zooming,

Five windup things,

Four crawling worms,

Three feather pens,

Two dancing gloves,

And a partridge in a square tree.

On the eleventh day of Christmas,

Louie gave to me

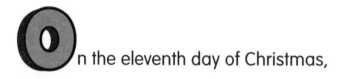

Ten brooms a-sweeping,

Nine spiders spinning,

Eight flowers singing,

Seven balls a-bouncing,

Six cars a-zooming,

Five windup things,

Four crawling worms,

Three feather pens,

Two dancing gloves,

And a partridge in a square tree.

On the twelfth day of Christmas,

friends all gave to me

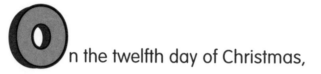

Eleven bells a-ringing,

Ten brooms a-sweeping,

Nine spiders spinning,

Eight flowers singing,

Seven balls a-bouncing,

Six cars a-zooming,

Five windup things,

Four crawling worms,

Three feather pens,

Two dancing gloves,

And a partridge in a square tree.

Merry Christmas!